Alfred Bull

Prudens Future

Alfred Bull

Prudens Future

ISBN/EAN: 9783337314590

Printed in Europe, USA, Canada, Australia, Japan

Cover: Foto ©Andreas Hilbeck / pixelio.de

More available books at **www.hansebooks.com**

PRUDENS FUTURI,

OR

Jaunts Off the High Road.

BY

ALFRED BULL.

PRIVATELY PRINTED

CHICAGO:

1891.

THIS BOOKLET
IS RESPECTFULLY DEDICATED TO THOSE
FRIENDS
WHOM IT MAY CONCERN.

PREFACE.

De Gusto Suo, said a sixteenth century philosopher when asked why he, instead of his adversary, had written a book, and certainly "to please one's self" is as good a reason as any other for print.

All have speculated on the Infinite; some to say with Bardolph, "Would I were with him, wheresome'er he is, either in heaven or in hell!" Others, like the hostess of the old Boar's Head Tavern in Eastcheap, may the rather say, "Now I, to comfort him, bid him 'a should not think of God; I hoped there was no need to trouble himself with any such thoughts yet."

Such thoughts were a part of my education, designedly clerical, but turned into other channels by the slow and costly process of acclimatization in "this busy perplexity of a New World," as Gerald Massey calls it. Enclosed cullings are from varied contributions to divers papers, the Presbyterian *Interior* and the Spiritualistic *Religio-Philosophical Journal* of this city, the *Spiritualist* of London, the *Harbinger of Light* of far Australia, the Chicago and Minneapolis *Tribunes*, various other secular papers, and from a projected book on "Heterodox Chicago." Pot-boilers have been rigidly excluded; the recital headed "Psychological" won a pleasing memento from Mr. Longfellow, and the "Narrative of Events about the

E Shaft," however incredible, is like all else herein, literally true.

The broadening tendency of modern religious thought is still insufficient to secure an open sesame to the columns of papers expounding special isms, unless their backs be scratched, and my *sow-wah* is too short to reciprocate; hence a seeming identification with spiritistic phases and journals, which implies a closer relation than really exists, although I gratefully acknowledge many courtesies from those sources.

· Preferring to use ears rather than tongue explains why these experiences will reach others in this form, when theirs have come to me rich and warm ifrom *viva voce* narration.

ALFRED BULL.

Chicago, December, 1890.

TABLE OF CONTENTS.

HETERODOX CHICAGO.

Wonderful stories had come to our ears of the sights to be seen, the sounds to be heard, by the expenditure of a solitary picayune at a weekly meeting held not a thousand miles from Chicago, where folks were said to "get" Spiritualism as others get religion. The rites of voodoo, howling dervishes, negro camp-meetings, all were cited as fit comparisons, and we determined to feel what it was to be there.

Over a sweltering stretch of knotty sidewalk we travel towards the setting sun, to eventually find ourselves in a cozy little hall, its pillars twined with tri-color, its proscenium flanked by extraordinary efforts at reproducing the human form, and surmounted by a quaint, frog-like figure, fit presiding genius of the exercises about to take place.

In an oval are arranged three rows of chairs forming the mystic "circle," seated thereon investigators into the harmonial philosophy. Well-developed heads are there, though here and there are visible startling facial angles, and abrupt transitions from eyebrows to hair that would warm the hearts of Darwinian philosophers.

Doctors without diplomas, professors filling no "chairs," mediums learned in every phase of spiritism abound. The music of the spheres is reproduced by a jangling pianoforte, and the chairman, middle-aged, complacent, self-satisfied, begins a narrative of his experience, in which spirit prophecies, the exhumation of dead bodies and instantaneous conversions figure.

The chairman seated, a pause ensues, until with peculiar swaying motion, and movements suggestive of partial paralysis or incipient epilepsy, which are common to nearly all the speakers who succeed her, there stands before us a gaunt, raw-boned woman, whose straggling hair, lack-luster eyes, and disjointed harangue, bring Meg Merrilies instantly before us. Scott's creation, however, possessed no substratum of emotional Methodism such as can be traced through her monotonous speech, and *ennui* has claimed us for its own, when

"Pop !" with Jack-in-the-box-like celerity, a little round-shouldered man is on his feet, and in thin, piping, nasal tones, whose rapid utterances are well-nigh unintelligible, holds us spell-bound by his extraordinary gesticulations until with a "pop." shrill and unexpected as the first, he subsides.

Long silence, a bland request from the chairman "not to fight off the influence, but to let it come," and a plump French woman, whose eyes twinkle with mirth behind her glasses, rises, and in a curious patois, redolent of slave-quarters, the backwoods, frontier and the slums, but which an initiated neighbor informs us is " Injun," speaks of the hereafter and her " control's " experience of it. A pause, a shrug and long-drawn sigh, and the volatile medium proceeds to declaim in slow measured words and purer English, as best seems to please the second spirit which now possesses her.

Her place is taken by a spare, dark man of severely intellectual appearance, who, with the same distressing abruptness, now holds forth in an unknown tongue.

" Greek ? " suggest we.

" Choctaw," says the initiated neighbor, but it is Greek to us.

Our Choctaw seats himself with a complacent smile ; a Welch woman, whose face recedes in beautiful perspective from that initial point, her nose, follows, is embarrassed, tries again, falters, engages " Pop " in a rambling conversation, and " the influence " leaves her.

After various false alarms, a lady is requested

to come to our aid, and kindly does so in an
oration of rare beauty, abounding in Christian
charity and delicate turns of thought.   She has
done, to our regret, and an immense female, whose
ample proportions are magnified by the strong
colors she wears, now has the floor.   She is " big
Injin chief, Chippewa," rejects with disdain the
sly · suggestion from a friend that all Indians
ought to be hanged, for says she, with greater
truth than she wots of "Chokum Chippewa, hur-
tum mejum squaw!". Her voice rises, her superb
animal organization responds, she (he) trundles a
mighty war whoop, and selecting an old foe in
the audience, holds him spell-bound by a torrent
of aboriginal invective, far more true to nature,
we fear, than ever Cooper was when he wrote of
the red men in the forest.

A suggestion is now started of a "chiel amang
us takin' notes."   Dismay succeeds, but the possibility of appearing in print is too great an in-
ducement for feminine vanity, the bait is taken,
and a tall, angular woman, carefully draping a
valuable shawl around her as she gets up, in-
dulges in dreamy abstractions and a mellifluous
conglomerate of absurdities touching upon life
beyond the grave.   Her wish is granted; may
she be happy.

Music again ; a hymn is sung, and a lusty Irishman, "a milkman, very bashful in the normal state," suavely requests permission "to take the flure." General expression of pleasure at the prospect following, a waltz is played, the "flure" taken, and our Irishman sails around the inner circle, cutting capers, jig-dancing, revolving in a manner wonderful to behold. A devil's tattoo is beaten by lively boot-heels upon the waxed floor, and in a few moments their fair owner is also on her feet, and pressing towards the center. Admitted, her clumsy movements grow rapid, the fun fast and furious ; her shawl falls, she doesn't heed it ; off goes her hat, on she goes ; and when, panting, she returns to her seat, with hair dishevelled and disordered dress, Paddy continues his airy gambols, fresh apparently as when first he "got " the influence.

A lady in the audience calls attention to the manner in which the woman danced, and the position in which she held her hands, deducing the fact that she must have had a spirit-partner, and henceforth this discoverer remains the center of an admiring group, is not without honor in her own country, and plumes herself upon the possession of spiritual vision.

The music ceasing, the meeting breaks up into

a general sociable, and eccentricity now has full play. Each speaker holds mimic court, and from every side float up scraps of conversation—" Me see um squaw over dere."—" I see a spirit standing by you."—" Your thinkum box,"—etc., a curious jumble. Little knots gather round the burning and. shining lights who now become prominent. Here a heavy-featured M. D., with a number of faded-looking women clucking in his train, suggests the barnyard king or the chief of a Salt Lake harem. There a little English woman betrays her monomania by occasional peals of laughter breaking strangely in upon the tale of domestic infelicity and confinement in a private asylum which she is pouring out to sympathetic ears. This lady is a fire-medium, hot and angry as the element she braves, as she describes her treatment by skeptics at a recent exhibit. Next her, a woman invites you to her rooms to witness divination by " tea-grounds," and one of her most interested auditors is a bony Hibernian, well advanced in years, about to drop into a fortune through a lapsed or missing will. The lights are now dimming, a communist has mounted a chair, and enunciates his peculiar views, and the proud possessors of a dozen proffered cards from professional clairvoyants, trance speakers, and others of that ilk, we make for the open air, and as our mystified brain resumes normal operations, conclude that there are more things in heaven, earth, and hell than were dreamed of in our philosophy.

JOTTINGS.

JOTTINGS.

Premising only that the following incidents are true, and have not heretofore been in print, let me first recite the substance of a conversation recently held with a gentleman well known in Chicago, and much farther afield, whom we will call, for purposes of non-identification, Mr. Si Loam.

"I am rather materialistic," began Mr. Loam, " and can explain to my own satisfaction whatever, seemingly abnormal, there may be in this experience. Some time ago, while engaged in literary work, which has since met with a cordial reception on both sides the Atlantic, I found work aggravatingly suspended by the loss of some important data—drafts, lists and other subject-matter—which my assistant insisted had been placed upon my desk, but which had mysteriously disappeared. Immediate search failed to discover them, and after frequent fruitless endeavors, the press of daily work put the matter temporarily aside, as no progress could be made in this particular until a large amount of preparation had again been undertaken, or the missing papers found.

"Three weeks passed, and one night, after a busy day occupied with routine and other issues, I went to bed to find myself presently unexpectedly wide-awake, and in a few minutes listening to a clock striking two. My thoughts were idle, my condition receptive, when a voice, distinct and clear, said to me, 'Si ! Si ! You'll find those missing papers back of the nest of drawers on the left hand side of your writing table.' 'Well,' said I, 'I am much obliged to you, whoever you are,' and in a few minutes was asleep again.

"Remembering this matter on waking, I resolved to test the statement that morning, but did not chance to have convenient opportunity until 4 p. m., when, calling my secretary, we unscrewed the top of my writing table, lifted it off, and I invited my assistant to reach down behind the nest of drawers ; down went his arm beyond the elbow, and up, to his delight, came the missing manuscripts. The voice ? Well, as real and material as any I have ever heard, and this was not the only time I had listened to it, always to find its assertions true.

"Oh ! you want my theory ? Here it is : Being a man of method, I make little allowance for, and permit no worry to disturb me, while I cannot afford to forget. Therefore I hold there is a

latent convolution of the brain, or independent
minor train of thought, which runs parallel with,
distinct from, and unnoticed by, the active ele-
ments, positive and in constant daily use. Having
instinctively delegated to it the search for the
missing papers much as one would say, 'Seek
him' to a retriever, this automatic action continued until, the discovery made, the clock-work
rumbled and whirred sufficiently loud to awaken
me and create the effect of audible speech. I
believe we all possess this faculty in greater or
less degree, and as already said, I have found it
very useful." Such automatic action might explain why tasks conned or committed to memory
over night are ordinarily better learned than if
the same task were attempted in the morning.

* * *

A fatal accident at a suburban station on the
C., B. & Q. R. R. the last summer was not unexpected by the lady thereby made a widow.
Disturbed by a clouded dream which left only a
sense of impending evil, she begged her husband,
while at breakfast, not to go to town that day;
but he ridiculed the idea, started, waited for one
train to pass, and crossed immediately behind it,
only to be cut down and mangled by a train un-
seen by him, going in a contrary direction. His

wife waited expectant at the door, and seeing the
crowd which had gathered at the depot, related
her conviction of her husband's death, before the
improvised stretcher emerged from among the
people and began its melancholy journey toward
her.

* * *

Reciting the above to a friend accidentally met
in a Chicago street-car, he told that three weeks
before a vivid dream had led him to fear an
accident to his mother, then far away. Misled
by his fears he overlooked the possibility of injury to any other, only to find, a few hours later,
that an almost equally dear mother by adoption,
his mother-in-law, had found her deafness fatal,
and was crushed by a C. & N. W. Railway suburban
train when but a few steps from home. "I
cannot say when," said this self-made, reliant,
representative Chicago business man, with, so far
as his friends know, no breath of superstition
about him, "but of this I am sure, our premo-
nitions will certainly become clearer, we shall
recognize the guiding hand, the element of chance
will be largely subordinated, and our lives will be
more fully rounded out." All hail the time when
no misdirected missive will go to the dead-letter
office.

Said another Chicago friend, a physician who has also done good work in other than a professional field: "My little girl who died last spring was strangely dear to me; my life seemed wrapped up in hers. Not approving of all evangelical methods, and opposed in many essentials to Sunday school ethics, I had carefully reared her according to my own conception of what is right, and kept well away from her any thought of sombre wrappings, a dismal tomb and repulsive decay. She knew of death only as a change of condition, a falling asleep, when the useless body was laid away, its work being done. So when I knew that she must die, she lay for the last thirty-six hours almost constantly in my arms, at her own dear request, not fearing, possibly little knowing, what the near future had in store. As the end drew nearer and was shadowed in her face, I rocked her gently to and fro, saying only, 'Go to sleep, dear, go to sleep, and all will be well.' Soon she fell asleep, and I have firm faith that all is well with her.' A pleasant attainment of that farther peak, beyond which lies eternity.

* * *

You have recently published interesting matter connected with the impressions of patients while under the influence of ether. Permit the space,

therefore, for the experience of a near relative
while comatose from ether in childbed. Her
recital is: "I lost all knowledge of my surround-
ings to speedily emerge into brillant sunlight,
changes of glorious light from moving boughs,
songs of birds, scents of gardens, woods and fields,
and walked elastic, rejoicing, along the Primrose
Way. I found myself suddenly confronted with
an impalpable shadow, yet seemingly dense, and
was filled with curiosity to face the mysteries
beyond this black opaque. With this determination I stepped briskly forward to find facing me
a gigantic, omnipotent-seeming eye, set in a circle
of quivering fire, and I heard a voice saying:
'Back! Go back! There is death beyond. Your
time has not yet come!' I turned, the eye dis-
appearing; returned, it again appeared; I urged
my wishes to meet only the same monition, and
was still vainly seeking a passage through this
vail, when called to earth by the quivering cry
of my little one, whose separate life was just
begun."

* * *

You have also given space to the alleged fatali-
ties and evil influences that overtook or enwrapped
those who were active in the prosecution to the
death of the fanatical lunatic, Charles J. Guiteau.

His execution chanced in my own honeymoon, spent at Riverside, and on my return from town —his late office and my own were in the same building—I was puzzled to find my young wife had shown her fealty to the tortured president, and her satisfaction at the law's supremacy, by constructing a quaint little dusky image, labelled Guiteau, which, with black cap duly drawn, hung by the neck and a cotton thread from a dwarf fuchsia in our parlor-window. Accepting, under protest, this temporary addition to our household gods, the matter was dismissed from our thoughts, and the next morning dawned in due course, the Fourth of July, 1882. A gentleman from town accompanied us in a stroll that afternoon around the peninsula formed by the Desplaines river, and we had occasional evidence that picnickers and others were enjoying the beauties of the woods, making merry in orthodox fashion with crack of cracker and rifle, and pistol bang. No one celebrating was within several hundred feet of us, as we walked three abreast, the wife in the middle, over the springy turf, when suddenly I heard the angry, spiteful hiss of a bullet beside my ear, and the "zip" of its blow, as it struck and fractured a garnet brooch on metal base worn by my wife on plaits of hair at the nape of her neck, and the ball then fell to the ground. Our plausible explanations received no heed, the messenger, fortunately a "spent-ball," told its own tale too plainly in bent and broken brooch and greasy, leaden traces on her finger-tips ; our walk was ended, and the lady hurried home to remove that wicked little effigy, which had been, somehow, she knew not how, the *deus ex machina* of this experience.

I am strongly tempted to run a tilt against some contributors who resemble the " thirty monstrous giants " described by Don Quixote, but remembering that his good lance was shivered, himself and Rosinante overthrown upon his first assault, I am reminded in season that the title " Religio-Philosophical " is very eclectic, your individual work and that of a majority of contributors excellent, and the space accorded to one necessarily limited.

PHENOMENAL.

PHENOMENAL.

NARRATIVE OF EVENTS THAT TOOK PLACE AROUND
THE E. SHAFT OF THE CHICAGO, WILMINGTON
AND VERMILLION COAL CO., IN BRAID-
WOOD, WILL CO., ILL., ON THE
NIGHTS OF AUGUST 14 AND
15, 1877.

PREAMBLE: Since the under-written phenomena are of a character sufficently remarkable and
abnormal to merit a careful recital and preserva-
tion, I take this earliest practicable opportunity
after their occurrence, while my recollection of
details remains minute, to record them for my
own satisfaction, and with a possible view to
publication in the interest of humanity and of
social science—with the proviso that up to the
date on which these incidents took place, my in-
vestigations into Spiritualism had only extended
to occasional seances with professional mediums;
and had resulted in the belief that the something
which had eluded my research might be the work
of a low order of spirits, might be the result of an
unknown power, often accompanied by trickery,

possessed in unequal degree by different individuals, who were usually of inferior moral, intellectual, or physical caliber.   With my position
towards Spiritualism defined, I now commence in
narrative form, a truthful and consecutive statement of events which occurred in my presence,
and in that of Mr.————, whose relatives reside in
New York (I withhold his name), on the nights
of August 14th and 15th, 1877.

On the afternoon of the first of August I received instructions to report for special duty at
Pinkerton's headquarters on Fifth avenue, Chicago, and a few hours later found myself comfortably housed in the police barracks extemporized
by the Chicago, Wilmington & Vermillion company upon their property in Braidwood.   The
position seemed to be a sinecure.

With some thirty-five others, I was detailed
upon guard at various points around the G and H
shafts with ample leisure for a scramble to "the
face" to see coal dug, to hunt for curious insects
or fossils.   Our occupation was rendered easy,
notwithstanding recent troubles with the strikers,
by the presence of Dwight, Streator and Pontiac
militia, by the enrollment and nightly drill of
some 250 colored "blacklegs" (miners who had
taken the place of strikers), and by personal as

surance from Gov. Cullom of his sympathy and material support.

Of my companions, one had provoked remark by preferring to spread his blanket under the open sky, beside piles of props, or in the engine-house, rather than share our common quarters; a man of some twenty-five years, ill-educated, dogmatic and taciturn, with a low forehead, sharp ridge-like eyebrows, restless, suspicious eyes, small pointed nose, hatchet-face, decidedly not an attractive companion with whom to share a night-watch. It was consequently with little pleasure that I learned from him of our having been detailed for night duty at the E shaft, half a mile from our headquarters, a couple of furlongs nearer town than our most advanced pickets were stationed. These reasons seemed sufficient to explain his statement that we had disagreeable work before us, and I was relieved to hear that the mine was exhausted, the shaft-house dismantled, and that three or four days would suffice to remove the debris and tools, when our services would no longer be required at that point.

I also learned that he had previously done night-duty on the same spot, as I buckled on my Remington, and with lunch and a blanket, we started for the scene of our labors at six o'clock

on the evening of the 14th. The allotment of
sleep had been left to our own discretion, and ac-
cordingly I turned in at dusk, while my comrade
watched, and was awakened by him at twelve to
exchange places.

The mine is located at the intersection of a
railroad with a thoroughfare which crosses it at
right angles. On the southern side of the railroad are scattered the diminutive clapboard
houses of the miners, each having a garden-patch,
and fronting on the highway. On the north side
of the track and along the eastern side of the road,
extend, fan-like, the tall crests and ravines of the
"dump," composed of shale and earth excavated
during five years of working; and at the handle
of the fan are located the main and ventilation
shafts, both partly filled with water and boarded
over, and the engine-house, of which the timbers
littered the ground, its tall iron funnel still standing and constituting with the brick work of the
furnace, and the boilers embedded in it, the only
portions of the house *in situ* north of the railroad; west of the road, its upper surface level
with it, extends a low flat dump of coal-dust and
earth partly covered with piles of hard-wood props,
by the iron-work of ruined "cages," dump cars and
debris. Near the road stands a tumble-down black-

smith shop, signs of decay in its iron-barred broken
windows, nailed-up doors, grimy cupola and
chimney, and battered, "holey" walls and floor.
It is unequally divided by a partition, the smaller
room containing the ash-covered forge, and the
more valuable parts of the wreck of the shaft-
house; the other room holding a rusty stove,
large heap of cable, picks and other tools, and an
old bench, upon which we spread our blanket.

Invigorated by sleep, I marched up and down,
until disturbed by rapid footsteps pacing to and
fro beyond the lower dump, and in a grass-grown,
boggy waste of five or six acres that stretched
north to an adjoining road. I followed cautiously,
hid, walked swiftly toward the sounds, but failing
to discover their source, finally contented myself
with listening carefully, and they continued at
intervals till daylight. About one o'clock, or a
little later I saw two lights upon the waste
referred to, four or four and a half feet from the
ground, dancing gaily up and down, approaching
and retreating, and wheeling round each other
like butterflies among flowers on a summer morning. Lanterns, some one after the wood, I thought,
as with ready revolver I chased them through
knotty grass, muddy bottom, and around the prop-
piles, but could not get within fifteen feet of them
despite my utmost efforts.

They were pale, shedding no radiance, wavering, flickering like a candle-flame in the wind, and of about four times the size. Suddenly, I thought I understood their nature, and, as Jack-o-lanterns or Will-o-the-wisps are only partial acquaintances of mine, strove more earnestly to make a near approach. Weary and baffled, I gave up the chase, and cannot tell the precise time of their disappearance.

"You don't want to go chasin' them lights," said one of our men at the breakfast-table, as I narrated my experience, and propounded my theory, shaking his head ominously, and proceeding to narrate some marvelous story of paralysis accompanying a near approach. Laughingly, yet half angry, I proposed on that evening to vindicate my theory, and effectually dispose of his superstitious views, but the dancing lights did not again appear.

Supper over, and on the ground again, the first watch fell to my lot, and my companion slept till midnight. Footsteps came again, faint and at distant intervals, but contenting myself with observing that all property was safe and in its place, twelve o'clock at last arrived, as Ursa Major's position indicated, and I awoke my comrade.

"Did you try to fool me during the night?" he asked.

"No. I have not been in the house till now."

"Some one seized my heel with both hands, and half-twisted my ankle. I woke up, saw you, I thought, standing beside me, and drew up my other foot, meaning to give you a kick that you would remember, if you tried it again; but I was tired and dropped off. And yesterday morning," he continued, " there came a tremendous thump, along about daylight, against the side of the house. I was asleep, but it startled me so that I woke sitting up. You didn't throw a stone against the house, did you?"

"1 heard that noise," I replied, "and hurried from the other end of the road, but could find nothing; looked through the window, saw you curled up, seemingly asleep, and concluded I must have been mistaken."

A little more chat, he closed the door, and I prepared to take off my shoes. As I did so, an unmistakable sigh came from the darkness, followed by a groan. I called my friend, again, and louder yet. He hurried up, and I questioned him as to trickery, which he solemnly denied.

Not feeling sleepy, and disliking my proposed couch, I volunteered to watch and let him continue his nap; but declining, we went out into the night.

The footsteps had become louder, and now as we listened, we could distinguish the measured tread of one pacing "sentry-go," the rush of many footsteps, the creaking of swift-moving boots. Search availed nothing, and sitting down chatting together, he spoke of being a fair singer, and I invited a specimen of his skill.

He broke off, as a dark shadow advanced swiftly towards us and disappeared. Soon from the opposite direction, it came again, a tall man, stooping, in dark clothes and slouch cap. My friend started up, and darted after it, slashing madly right and left with his cudgel as he raced over the low dump, while I followed, pistol in hand. Suddenly we stopped; it had disappeared, in clear starlight on the open dump.

Singing resumed, my "butty's" repertoire (of the varieties order) nearly exhausted, his songs became more vulgar and obscene until, in the last, he broke off; for the footsteps had become fearfully loud and near, were all around us, on the low dump, the road, the gritty railroad track, and with them came the sound of the pick "at the face," of the shovel as "the rooms" were cleaned out, and of miners busily at work; while from the blacksmith-shop came loud raps and knocks.

"Did you hear those three loud knocks?" And

my "yes" was emphasized by another rap louder still.

I started to my feet.

"We will go into that shop together, and find out what it is," said I.

After some hesitation he consented. We went hand in hand. In the name of God, I demanded was there some suffering, evil or unhappy spirit present, who needed our help. No reply, no sound came.

"If you cannot answer that, you must be imps of the devil," I exclaimed.

At that, my friend snatched his hand from mine, flew into the open air, and I followed.

"What made you run?" I asked.

"You don't want to talk about the devil in there."

"Perhaps not. But we will find some other reason yet."

"You can't do it. I've been here three weeks, and there's no other man on our force dare stay here. They'd take their walking papers first. Kennedy was with me, and he could not stand it, and left. They take me to the edge of that shaft, eighty-five feet deep, and tell me to throw myself down." As he spoke, he walked towards the spot, picked up a piece of coal, dropped it between the boards; we listened to the echoing plunge, and walked away. Then resuming, " I've lost eighteen pounds since I've been at it."

" Do these sounds follow you? Have you heard them anywhere else?" I asked.

" No. But—I have been dead once! I was drowned! It was an awful warning! My grandfather died six times!"

This calmly, deliberately, solemnly, his face rigid in the starlight, at a time when the presence of a human being became valuable; for the sounds were louder, nearer, menacing. Dogs (every miner keeps one) were howling fearfully.

The eaves of the shop, its cupola and chimney were faintly luminous, phosphorescent; far off on the horizon the light of some burning house, barn, or prairie shone, but the coming dawn we had noticed a short time before seemed overclouded, the air murky, dark, and stifling. Whether this effect was real, or within ourselves, I do not know. Both had remarked it, we found afterwards.

I felt the reflection of a light on my face, and, turning quickly, saw a ball of fire fall, splash like molten iron on the road beside me, but without sound, and disappear.

" Did you see it as it passed your face? "

" No," said I, "I did not."

" It was a finger of fire, and was shaken in your face! I never saw them so near before, nor heard them so loud." Then after a long pause : " Can you pray? "

" I don't know," I said. " I never prayed with anyone before, but I must try."

" Won't you kneel down?" he asked.

" I do not think God cares about position, but I will," and hand in hand again, I prayed, "making the best prayer that ever I heard," said my companion.

" Now," said I, "let us repeat together the Lord's prayer."

" I don't know it," he replied.

So I said it for both.

As we rose, all was peaceful, the silence startling by comparison with the babel that had gone before. The sky had cleared, and the victory was ours. Speaking of the wonders of the night, and our happy release, my companion chanced to drop a familiar oath, and the sound of the footsteps, the pick, the shovel, the knocks began again. I rebuked him; they died away; in an hour daylight had come, and we turned toward the shop. The door we had returned after our flight to close stood wide open, the loose coils of rope had been

removed diagonally to the opposite corner, and
were heaped at the end of the bench.

We searched the low dunes, the dumps, the
field, no trace of shifted soil or any alteration,
where the noise had been loudest. I looked for
any indication that gravitation might have restored the angle of repose—the dumps were below
it, and no indication of a slide appeared; for any
sign in nature or man, for a trace of the rope,
anything to account for these phenomena on ex-
plainable principles, I could not find any. Then
I turned in for an hour, was awakened by our
relief, and made our report to the sergeant. He
God-d——d my ghosts, my prayers, my report,
but at noon apologized; excused himself on the
score of fatigue after a night ride for a physician,
and on the momentary supposition that I had in-
tended a practical joke.

The men listened intently, and from them I
now learned, for the first time, that on the 13th
of August, nine years previously, a picnic had
been held at that spot; there was a strike at the
time, quarrels began, and ended in the murder of
a number of men. How many, the different nar-
rators differed too much upon for me to deter-
mine. Confirmation of my companion's statement regarding them was also furnished.

I gave my companion, at his request, the Lord's prayer, in writing and print with an alphabet for each, and he expressed his intention of learning it. Both looked forward to the evening with a courage born of our experience, that surprised our comrades; but, as I was lying down in the afternoon, the sergeant brought me a telegram from Chicago:

"Come at once; I want to place you on another operation."

Said the Sergeant, "No doubt the superintendent, who signs this, wants you on the clerical force or on private work. If the latter, your apparent connection with the force will cease; therefore, no word to the men, and take first train up."

I presented myself in Chicago.

"What about the E shaft?"

Then I perceived that the "operation" was to be performed on myself.

"Who was with you?"

I made a brief report. He noted the name.

"Ah!" sad smile. "I don't think I will send you down there again."

"Did I not do my duty?"

Significant tap of the side of his head, repetition of smile, finally:

"It has a tendency to demoralize the men."

"You have other work?" I asked.

"What is your opinion about the E?"

"That I was further within the gates of hell there than I thought it possible for man to go, and be alive."

"No further work," said the superintendent.

"In that case, these experiences are mine alone, and I am free to make what use of them I please," from me closed the interview.

I paid a visit to the superintendent of the C. W. & V. Co. He had neither leisure nor inclination for investigation.

THE HICKSITES.

THE HICKSITES.

Hicksites? A branch of the Quakers, was my mental query and response, but as I enter the comfortable class-room to find the Friends hatless, the sexes not separated, but few distinctions in dress or colors, I am disposed to question my information.

We are seated, a score of us, the hour advertised has arrived, yet apparently the services have not commenced. Facing us at a plain table are three friends, with no outward show of heteroclitic or heretical belief, three unassuming gentlemen; and as the minutes creep slowly past, I resign myself to the pleasant influences of the hour, oblivious of the outer world save as the jingle of a passing street-car, the beat of a distant snare-drum, or a buzzing fly, recall my vagabond thoughts.

Half an hour has slipped away when one of the trio, a well-known wholesale dealer, rises, expresses his gratitude for the opportunity afforded us of gathering for public worship, sitting in silence of body, our minds withdrawn from all thoughts not having a bearing upon our duty to

God or our fellow-men, and endeavoring to bring
our spiritual nature into the ascendency, and a
nearness to the Great Spirit. This will lead us
into a sense of our own spiritual needs, he tells
us, cause prayer or asking for what we lack, and
if it lead us into supplication it will be with
fervent power, and the souls of those gathered
will feel its warmth and genuineness. Sitting in
humbleness of spirit, waiting upon the giver of
spiritual sight and blessing, all, educated and
uneducated, rich and poor, robust and feeble, can
feel the fellowship of brethren under a realization
of the Fatherhood of God. The fever-heat gener-
ated at the outbreak of our civil war, gradually
merging into steady determination, and strenuous,
contained effort; the cool bravery of a policeman
in entering, single-handed, a struggling crowd of
lawless men, upheld in his duty by the recognized
majesty of the law, are cited as examples and
illustrations in the daily battle of life, and the
speaker has done.

But he has been too warlike, has disturbed the
peaceful breast of an aged sister, clad in orthodox
Quaker garb, and she takes up the gauntlet.
Severely simple in appearance, the folded white
neckerchief, tunnel-like bonnet, and black gown,
suggest a time when these premature cerements

shall be applied to real use, the hard lines in that
worn face fade away, and the sweet smile, temporarily banished by ascetism, which we know
to be behind those trembling lips, come to the
surface, a pleasant aftermath for sorrowing friends
to gather.

She speaks with a strong German accent; her
address is stereotyped, as she dwells upon the
biblical injunctions to turn the other cheek when
one is smitten, of awarding good for evil, and
urges upon us that patient endurance attaineth to
all things. Stereotyped and a well-conned and
oft-repeated lesson, yet well in accord with this
sweet Sabbath stillness. The first speaker kneels
and offers an earnest prayer for divine guidance;
noon has come, notices of the classes to succeed
are read, the infant class, that engaged in studying James Freeman Clarke's "Ten Great Relig-
ions," and one upon "Communism." The leader
shakes his neighbor's hand devoutly, who in turn
greets his silent friend, the meeting is adjourned,
and curious to know how Quakers are affected by
the cry of liberty, equality, fraternity, we follow
to the adjoining class-room.

The principal speaker again leads, reads from
the prospectus of the National Labor League, and
from the speech of one of its most ardent ad-

vocates, general discussion is invited and ensues. An expected reading from Ruskin is missing, general want of preparation urged, the conclusion that selfishness is at the root of the matter, and its cure to be found in understanding that true theology is practical righteousness arrived at, and the subject deferred for future consideration.

By the courtesy of the leader I learn the real points at issue between the Wilburite, Gurneyite, Hicksite factions of the Society of friends, learn that the old objections to oath-taking, to titles, hat-raising still exist, but that theater-going, card-playing, dancing, music, statuary and decorations in members' houses are practically condoned by tacit consent. The ordinance against them remains an unwritten law, and while excess is condemned, healthy and temperate indulgence in innocent pleasure is encouraged by many.

The formal thee and thou are generally used by Hicksites in communication with the outside world, except by younger members, the rigid laws anent the marriage relation modified, the spirit considered more, the letter worshiped less. Women are admitted to all the privileges, positions and duties of the body, including eldership and ministry. Elias Hicks' name is not accepted authoritatively, but only his views upheld so far as he protested against threatened credal bonds, in much the same way as the majority of New Church members regard Swedenborg.

They do not undervalue the fullest preparation for ministerial duty by study of the Scriptures, by meditation, by acquaintance with human nature as manifested in themselves or others, and with science in all its branches, and by the wise use of all their faculties in gaining knowledge and broadening their perceptions of truths, but ask, that as the minister or disciple of Christ sits in the place of public worship, his or her mind may be gathered into stillness away from human will-ings, so that the divine spirit may be felt im-pressing it with the particular truth needed then, and which God alone can qualify us to unerring-ly see, or give the ability to present in convicting power.

The Bible they accept as being the Jewish in-terpretation and record of God's will and dealing towards men and nations, setting forth in the light they were capable of receiving, the divine truth known to the Jews in the ages of which it bears record. They think the Word of God to be his spiritual voice speaking in the soul, and do not use the term in speaking of the Bible. They believe, however, that the Word of God inspired the Bible writers with a sense or knowledge of the truths they wrote of, and in this meaning accept their writings as sacred Scripture.

Difficult as it is to quote the general belief of a sect strenuously opposed to the formulation of its opinions into a creed, we may accept as representative the views of the Trinity approved and printed by the Illinois yearly meeting of Friends at their session last year.

"We believe there is but one God, and that he is the Father, Cause or Creator, primarily, of all things, and the continual source or fountain of spiritual truth, light or power. Being spiritual in character, we know him only through his works in the material world, and thus the spirit in us receives the divine teachings, gains experience in divine knowledge, and is enabled to comprehend his nature, recognize his laws and present them to the intellectual comprehension through the connection of the spirit and mind.

"Christ we acccept as the Son of God, having all power from the Father. As God is a spirit, his Son must be spiritual, like begetting like. As manifested in fullness of power in the pure and perfect humanity of Jesus of Nazareth, He came to close the old dispensation of priests and outward ordinances of human intercessors with

tithes and sacrifices, and to usher in the full and
purer dispensation of God as a direct teacher of
each soul through Christ, his Son, the inward
light of that soul.

"God's power is also manifested through the
Holy Ghost or Spirit, as a sudden and thorough
revealer of our errors and sinful estate, overwhelm-
ing us with a sudden sight of our condition, followed by a change of heart.

"Again, as a light or sense, enabling the receiver
to see into or feel the state of other souls, and
giving power to effectively reach them with God's
convicting truth. And, lastly, as a Comforter,
keeping them true and filling them with ecstatic
joy in the midst of great trials or terrible tor-
tures. Distinguished from Christ, the gentle,
the ever-present leader and inward revealer, by
being God's light and power manifested upon
pressing occasion, in an especial manner and with
unusual and convicting clearness and force;
Ghost meaning vehemence."

PSYCHOLOGICAL.

PSYCHOLOGICAL.

The succeeding narrative, necessarily restricted
where it touches upon the soul-life, "the holy of
holies," of those still living, is submitted without further criticism than is furnished by the following extract from a private letter:

NEW YORK, May 16th, 1877.

DEAR SIR:—I have been very much interested in the
notes you have forwarded to me * * * Whether
they are veritable history or imagination, they are valuable
material—especially valuable in their suggestions The
adoption into the life of beautiful ideals in place of God,
or in lack of God, and getting an impulse to goodness from
them, is a unique process quite worthy of the attention of
the psychologist * * *   J. G. HOLLAND.

Some years since I came to this country a
stranger; far from all I loved, and unsuccessful
at first, longing for home and sympathy, having
only the stars in common with my friends (and
not all of them), there insensibly grew up in my
mind a morbid self-pity that alarmed yet comforted me; then mobile imagination served me in
good stead, making of rare meals of bread and
cheese dainties fit for the gods, gilding enforced
nightly wanderings through more than one of our
great eastern cities with a touch of romance, and

making many bitter experiences while roving from New England to the Gulf of Mexico, and up and down the Mississippi, the "great river," all subordinate to a romance that I was weaving and living.

Haunted by a poem of Longfellow, "The Two Locks of Hair," I united the loving companionship of one dear friend with the idealized beauty of another, the name of a third and a romantic meeting with a fourth, and blending into one harmonious whole their various accomplishments, with the chivalrous devotion to women my mother had taught me, thought much of my past life, and fell to musing on the virtual death an *emigree* suffers when he leaves all he loves behind him.

Gradually there crept into the aching void that my life knew, a fantasy that took tangible shape. I imagined that I had lost a wife, that our little one was ailing, and passed unscathed through many "trials and tribulations," upheld by a determination to be worthy of this shadowy past, to be true to the memory I had created (it pains me even to allude to my ideals as wholly imaginary), and encouraged to persevere in securing to my non-existent little one a thorough education and a cheerful home.

Although I knew that this was harmful, even dangerous, I seemed to derive real strength and comfort from the thought, and having what, at that time I was without—something to live for —insensibly it became a part of my nature, and fact and fancy so closely welded, that I found it difficult to realize I had possessed no wife, no little one; that these phantoms with which I was sharing my life, had no existence, save as they might foreshadow a happy future.

So the purely ideal angel companionship I had created became an actual part of my every day life. Vile dens, loathsome company, continued ill-fortune, were set at naught.

Finally, as circumstances improved, I dreaded the morbid tendency, and submitted the heads of this hallucination to a physician. He couched in pompous, technical language his real ignorance: "Morbid sensibility unduly exciting the imagination, consequent on lack of proper nourishment;" but from my father came a curious suggestion:

"The case, viewed metaphysically, appears to me a remarkable instance of the transmission of a mental impression from father to son, modified by circumstances, and intensified by want of sufficient nourishment. From the latter cause the vital force would be unequally distributed, and retiring from the stomach and digestive organs, might be expected to concentrate in the brain.

"When your sister was taken from us in infancy, I indulged in the hope that she would go to be with a dear, dead friend; that the latter would be a mother to the little stranger and introduce her among the angels. While my mind was filled with these ideas, you made your advent into the world. Your phantom wife and child seem to me but these two reproduced as the result of a mental impression of which you were the recipient before you came into the world.

"At the same time, may they not have been really with you, striving, by intensifying the impression, to shield you from harm?

"I have long believed in the existence of such impressions derived from parents as a fact, but never met with so direct a confirmation as your experience furnishes."

In conclusion, since ideas communicated orally or in writing, are never received in the precise form in which they are given, so with regard to impressions more purely mental, the recipient subject necessarily modifies, reproduces them in an altered form; and shall I, a child in matters anent spiritualism, can I do otherwise than echo Col. John Hay's words:

"I think that saving a little child,
And bringing him to his own,
Is a darned sight better business
Than loafing around the throne."

EXPERIENCES OF THE SPIRIT
IN DREAMLAND.

EXPERIENCES OF THE SPIRIT IN DREAMLAND.

Permit me to add my mite to the regret, expressed so universally by legal, scientific and spiritualistic journals throughout the English speaking world, at the sudden death of the eminent jurist, Mr. Serjeant Cox.

I first met him when assisting at an entertainment in Silchester Hall, London, some twelve years ago, at which meeting the Serjeant presided. His easy good-nature, and interest in all designed for the general weal, had led him on a comfortless winter night, many miles from his own luxurious fireside, to preside at this meeting in a squalid, rawly-new suburb, attended by its poverty-stricken inhabitants, at a nominal admission fee. And it is of painful interest to note in this connection that the attack to which he succumbed immediately succeeded his exertions consequent on a similar philanthropic effort.

Through subsequent correspondence, favors granted me when, as honorary secretary of a similar series of entertainments, I needed his

services, and an earnest interest in his doings as
successively chronicled in the daily press, I
learned to appreciate his large-heartedness and
powers of keen, critical analysis; and rejoiced
with him as he slowly emerged by laborious and
patient experiment, heedless of contumely, pity
or superficial ridicule, from the shadows of
"psychic force" to the purer light of Spiritualism.

Such a heart and brain as his are letters-
patent to any movement, and his painstaking
efforts in connection with the meetings of the
Dialectical Society, his establishment of the
Psychological Society, and energetic, long-con-
tinued advocacy of the truth, have won for him
such a place among spiritualistic pioneers in
England as is accorded to Judge Edmonds here.
While he had achieved three-score years and ten,
his ever active interest in contemporary litera-
ture, and in all the varied subjects to which he
gave careful attention, rendered his sudden death
an unwelcome surprise to all, and England cannot immediately fill his vacant chair.

Venturing over the same path he trod so
firmly, purveying as does the jackal for the lion,
thankful as I am if, after all psychic, odic, mes-
meric and magnetic aura are learnedly distilled,

enough remains for a meal, allow me again to offer the singular experiences of some friends in dreamland and *terra incognita*. As the experiences of Chicago people, possessing only a sneaking kindness for Spiritualism, notwithstanding the experience they themselves have had, though one rise from the dead they will not believe, I am compelled to omit all proper names and data that would lead to identification. Consequently I can only offer my own faith in their veracity, after having striven to exhaust all normal theories, Spiritualism and her sisterhood apart.

* * *

A real-estate dealer in this city, formerly resident in a neighboring county, had the misfortune to lose his wife, to whom he was devotedly attached, and, being of skeptical tendencies, having no faith in a life beyond this, a blank void spread before him from which his very soul recoiled. Months passed, and he had become morose, desolate, his business neglected, his friends estranged, the lunatic asylum yawned wide open for him, when, one summer evening, near dusk, he started for a lonely stroll.

As his garden gate clicked behind him, an arm was gently linked in his own, and turning he saw his dearly-loved wife again beside him, gazing

into his face with tender solicitude. Mechanic-
ally, doubting his own senses, he turned to begin
his stroll, but she accommodated her pace to his,
and leaning lovingly on his arm, the familiar ac-
cents again met his ears, and for an hour he
listened, in ecstatic delight, to an earnest, holy
exposition of his duties, too sacred for repetition.

Meanwhile they had traced together the round
he had designed, each avoiding irregularities in
the path, making due divergence necessary from
building materials at one point; and save that
her step was lighter, and her motion more like
that of floating than ordinary locomotion, he
could detect no other changes, could only realize
that the dreary interval had been bridged, and
she was again beside him, the dread future vanished. They had met no one on the walk, and as
they paused for a moment at the gate, the loving
pressure lightened, was gone, and she had disappeared, while on his lips trembled the thousand
things he had desired to say, and into his heart
came, and took root, permanent knowledge of the
truth that "blessed are they that mourn, for they
shall be comforted."

* * *

I turn now to three incidents in the life of a
city merchant, an old man racked with uncer-

tainty as to the journey in the dark so soon to be undertaken.

Thirty-five years ago, a callow youth, in all the agonies of calf-love, he misunderstood the symptoms, proposed too soon to the wrong lady, when one in the same house had really won his heart. On the bridal morning, he was giving his boots their final polish before the ceremony, when the latter lady came into the room. A brief conversation led to the final statement, "If you say yes—down go the boots." But she understood her position better than he, and urged him to do his duty as she understood it. In a short time she also married, and died in giving birth to a child. My friend subsequently paid a visit to the widower, and occupied the bed in which she had died. He was awakened by an impression of her bodily presence, and, though seeing nothing, folded her in his arms, and they held converse through the night. The morning found him a new man, his dormant duty to the woman he had sworn to love awakened, and her life, till its close, the happier for the factor which had previously been lacking.

This may seem decidedly sentimental, and yet had you seen the odd intensity of this practical, satirical old man, as his memory, moved by some accidental trigger, recalled the scene, no one could doubt his own firm belief in its reality, while the contrast with his every-day life such an incident affords strengthened its probability and its influence with him.

Twenty years ago he retired to rest without thought of his daughter, a thousand miles away, but awoke in the morning to tell his wife he had dreamed of their child's serious illness, and of the alarm he felt. The impression remained, notwithstanding all efforts at sober daylight thought, and in the afternoon came a dispatch: "Your daughter is seriously ill. Diptheria." The next day she was dead.

The last of his experiences, as related to me, was an incident occurring only five months since. A servant girl had recently been married at his house, and, removing about half a mile, had gone to housekeeping. Working far away from home, the girl's full heart had naturally been poured out to her kind mistress, and the ties of sympathy were close and strong. One afternoon the lady, seated by her window, heard the girl call her shrilly and suddenly; dismissed for a time the idea, but disagreeably impressed by it, finally prepared for walking, and arrived at her humble friend's home to find the latter, then in feeble health, extended on the floor in a dead faint. On recovering, the girl admitted having called on her former mistress' name when first seized, though the distance and multitudinous noises of a great city effectually prevented her cry from being heard even by neighbors or passers by.

* * *

Four years ago a hotel-keeper of Minneapolis, Minn., Aralzeman Bacon by name, whom I had known long and intimately, died, a free-thinker with disregarded spiritualistic tendencies. Shortly before his death he told me of the premonition he had received of his brother's death, when both were boys. Mr. Bacon, then seventeen years old, and living on his father's homestead on the Connecticut river, one afternoon, during his brother's absence with New York friends, fell without warning in a fainting fit on the kitchen floor. Reviving, he described the capsizing of a boat in which his brother and a party of friends were sailing, and the death by drowning of the former. Although entirely ignorant of his brother's doings on that day, subsequent letters detailed the accident with its fatal result, in exact accordance with his description; the time of the one's swoon, the other's death exactly coincided.

In conclusion, my mother furnishes me with an interesting incident in the life of a lady friend who was possessed of unusual mental and physical attractions. Advised by mutual friends not to broach the subject of Spiritualism with Mrs. M. (as we will call her), the subject tabooed was eventually introduced by that lady herself.

Her eager questionings won equally earnest responses, and led to the narration of the following experience in Mrs. M.'s life. While her mother was on her deathbed she had informed her daughter, Mrs. M., of the disposition she desired to make of certain jewelry, and its proper distribution among her children; but after the funeral, this property fell into the hands of another daughter, who, in the absence of legal proof to the contrary, appropriated it. So matters remained for three months, when this sister wrote Mrs. M. the particulars of a dream she had had the previous night, in which her mother appeared, and stated that her wishes with regard to the jewelry would be found written on the back of an oil painting, then in Mrs. M.'s house.

The picture had been sent to a cleaner a few days before, but happily was secured untouched; while the paper, soiled and discolored, but legible, was discovered on the back, confirming in its provisions the prophetic dream.

* * *

Are such experiences proofs of immortality, or must we fall back on the new-old theories of sympathy, and lapsed memory unconsciously restored, to explain them? Here be texts, let who will preach the sermon. Those who may remember some extraordinary experiences of mine at Braidwood, Ill., in August, 1877, duly detailed at that time, may be interested to hear of an agreement I have made with a noted "spirit exposer" to revisit the mines there and spend the anniversary on the spot together. If he keep his appointment, there may be a sequel to that story.

THE DISCIPLES OF CHRIST.

THE DISCIPLES OF CHRIST.

Some months. since I attended a meeting of the Disciples of Christ to find myself utterly alone in that little gathering, for the members on that occasion were Danes, and the language in which the services were conducted was Danish; but managing to follow the discussion which an incursion of Baptists and Pedobaptists had precipitated, I discovered so much of a character opposed to my preconceived ideas of Campbellism as to decide on repeating the call. I learned, incidentally, that notices of the services are published in Scandinavian as well as English journals, and that though usually conducted in English, the interests of the majority are considered in deciding which language shall be used.

On my second visit to the little frame house in which the meetings are held, I was more fortunate. It was early, yet within the little sitting-room five people were assembled, earnestly discussing, Bible in hand, various doctrinal points. The table, something of unknown shape upon it covered with a white table-cloth, exercised my ingenuity in vain.

Seating ourselves in a circle round the table, a hymn is sung, its peculiar intonation and interminable length bridging a score of years, so vividly does it recall meetings of the Plymouth brethren in London, of which such hymns were a prominent feature. At its close a prayer is offered, during which all kneel, another hymn is sung, the eleventh chapter of the First Epistle to the Corinthians read, with special reference to the communion we are about to receive, the cloth raised, disclosing a square soda-cracker and glass of wine, of which all in turn partake. A chapter is now read, a verse by each, and exegesis, in which figures prominently a Cruden's concordance, follows.

There is a studied informality about the exercises which is not displeasing. I am encouraged to ask for information as to this wheel within a wheel, these Disciples of Christ who advertise their meetings under that name, yet are at variance with the sect called by it and more widely known as Campbellites.

I learn that they are one in rejecting creeds as bonds of fellowship, and in disapproval of the technical language of popular theology, the use of such terms as trinity, eternally-begotten, co-essential and consubstantial.

The "Church of Christ," "Christian Church," or "Disciples of Christ" (Campbellites), organized on an evangelical basis, has elders, deacons, and evangelists or missionaries, stipulates only for one faith, one Lord, one immersion, one hope, one body, one spirit, one God and Father of all; recognizes the obligation to provide for the teaching of the gospel as of the greatest importance, and is one with evangelical Christians in its views of the atonement, the resurrection, and the future judgment.

The Disciples of Christ who form this little company, with another in Illinois, one in Indiana, a few scattered along the Eastern seaboard, and in Europe, accept that title alone; and are singular in tracing their origin, not from the time of the Campbells' rupture with the "Seceders," or subsequently with the Redstone Baptists, but back to the time of Christ himself.

They claim to rely wholly upon the Bible and individual inspiration resulting from its careful and prayerful study, yet with curious insistency profess to be more in accord with Alexander Campbell's teachings than is the sect known by his name, with one important difference. They believe with him that all Scripture given by inspiration of God is profitable for teaching, for

conviction, for correction, for instruction in righteousness, that the man of God may be perfect
and thoroughly accomplished for all good work;
in one God, as manifested in the person of the
Father, of the Son, and of the Holy Spirit, who
are one, therefore, in nature, power and volition:
that every human being participates in all the
consequences of the fall of Adam, and is born
into the world frail and depraved in all his moral
powers and capacities, so that, without faith in
Christ, it is impossible for him, while in that
state, to please God.

They believe that the Word, which from the
beginning was with God, and which was God,
became flesh and dwelt among us as Emanuel or
God manifest in the flesh, and made an expia-
tion of sin by the sacrifice of Himself, which no
being could have done who was not possessed of
superhuman, superangelic and divine nature.

They agree with Dr. Campbell in the justification of a sinner by faith without the deeds of the
law, and of a Christian, not by faith alone, but
by the obedience of faith: in the operation of the
Holy Spirit through the Word, but not without
it, in the conversion and justification of the sinner. Also in the right and duty of exercising
our own judgment in the interpretation of the

Holy Scriptures; in the authority and perpetuity of baptism, and the weekly administration of the Lord's Supper, which, they contend, has the warrant of apostolic example, and is therefore of divine obligation, and they say that it was the principal motive for the meetings of the first Christians on the Lord's Day, and for the peculiar sanctification of that day.

But they do not believe in the divine institution of the evangelical ministry, will accept no form of church government save that of elders who are old in wisdom and experience, build no churches, gather at each other's houses, and hold that baptism is immersion.

"By whom are you baptized?" I ask.

"By any one, by you as well as another," and, pleased at the interest displayed, hopeful of a convert, the boatman tells of his twenty-five-mile walk to and from the nearest water when he was baptized. Other experience succeeds, a hymn is sung, and, all rising, receive the benediction.

A HAUNTED HOUSE.

.

A HAUNTED HOUSE.

The following narration has long been a matter of oral tradition in my family circle, and may interest a larger audience:

" When I was about five years old, my father purchased some old houses in a small market town of Gloucestershire, England, one of which we occupied. The former tenants were known to my mother, but had died shortly before. No sooner were we settled down than my parents' sleep was disturbed by a ceaseless pattering over the boards in the bedrooms, as if a little bare-footed child were running up and down. Waking up at the noise, my father would leap from bed and chase the flying footsteps, always to stop, baffled, at the head of the stairway, where they suddenly ceased. As both he and his wife were what would now be called mediums, and had received equally curious testimony of the life immortal in the past, they became gradually accustomed to the footsteps, and attributing them to a spiritual source, ceased to notice them except by a passing remark.

" Some months passed, and one bright summer morning, following my usual custom, I left my bed to nestle beside my mother and the baby. It may have been about six o'clock, the sun was shining brightly in at the windows, and I had scarcely settled myself comfortably in place, when I saw a woman standing by the left-hand side of the bed. Jumping to the conclusion that my eldest sister was playing a joke upon me, and with childish glee at my own quick comprehension, I slipped my right hand from under the clothes, ready to catch hold of her as she neared me. Never moving my eyes from the figure, I watched it as, coming slowly down that side, and rounding the foot, it turned, showing the full face, that of a stranger, and came slowly toward my trembling, outstretched hand, which I was too terrified to withdraw, when it suddenly vanished. A thin, spare face, with sharp, pinched nose, eyes deep-sunken and set in heavy shadows, dark hair braided on the forehead. Sixty years have passed since I saw it, multitudes of other faces have come between that time and the present, but my recollection of it is clear as if seen but yesterday. Dressed as it was in a long white nightgown, a cap with deep full border, and with a white handkerchief tied under the jaws, coming a little over the chin, I had no fear nor conception of death at that time, yet well remember burying my head under the coverlet, while all the answer my mother could get from me was, 'I saw a woman! I saw a woman!'

"But as my first blind terror passed, my mother coaxed me to describe the figure, and said to a neighbor, 'Yes, it was Mrs. Cole.' This was the name of the old tenant, and a story was whispered in the town of her past cruelty to an orphan nephew, who had died in childhood in that house, leaving her heiress to the property he would have enjoyed, had he lived. Association of ideas and rumor alike suggest that he had been shut up, starved and beaten in those upper rooms, and when trying to escape, naturally sought flight by the stairway.

"Fifteen years passed, the family circle was broken; death, marriage and distant pursuits, had left my mother alone in the old home, when awakening early one morning, she saw the same woman, dressed as when I beheld her, seated on the side of the bed, the cap border crushed as if the head had just been lifted from the pillow Intently regarding her, my mother then turned her back on the unwelcome visitor, and prayed that she might be removed. Looking round again, she was gone.

"I believe the poor unhappy spirit was earthbound, doomed herself to wander about the room in which she had caused the little innocent child to suffer. The miserable expression of that face, its appearance of profound sorrow, is a mournful memory, yet I often recall it with feelings of deep thankfulness; considering it a great privilege, in this age of doubt and skepticism, to have looked upon a disembodied spirit, face to face."

ELIZABETH BULL.

London, England.

A Strange Manifestation.

A STRANGE MANIFESTATION.

I was sitting in my room, my oldest boy (now 40 years of age) a baby on my lap, a servant engaged in removing the tea things, and, feeling very happy, I was humming a tune. Suddenly I noticed in a corner of the room a small mass of misty whiteness. Shaking my finger warningly at the girl to silence her, and looking intently at this strange object, it rapidly increased in size until several feet in height; growing gradually dense and more opaque, and slowly opening, it revealed the glorified form of my dear sister. I say glorified, since language utterly fails to convey any idea of that lovely, wondrous vision.

She had died in her twenty-third year of lingering consumption, ten years before; and had borne great suffering with Christian fortitude, joyfully looking for speedy release. Unselfish and lovable, a beautiful soul fitly clothed, she gradually wasted under the fell disease, and died at length in my arms. But now I saw her again—all traces of lingering disease had vanished, she looked radiantly beautiful as, holding back the surrounding envelope, she leaned towards me, the dear, sweet eyes gazing into mine with a look of unutterable love. She wore a long, loose robe of dazzling whiteness, hanging about her in graceful folds, and there emanated from her a mellow, soft light, making the encrusting shell glitter like crystal. So gloriously beautiful was the appearance that I could not gaze upon it without pain, nor do I think that natural eyes could have seen it; but so soon as I had thoroughly realized this angelic presence she gradually drew the encircling mass about her, and ever steadfastly regarding me, was gradually hidden from view, the luminous envelope clouded, darkened slowly, shrank, and disappeared.

My incoherent exclamations of delight and wonder frightened the girl, who had seen nothing save my own wrapt gaze; but I had seen my sister, and I shall see her again in our heavenly home, where there is no more sorrow, no more parting, no more death.

ELIZABETH BULL.

London, England.

THE CHRISTADELPHIANS AND THE DARBYITES.

THE CHRISTADELPHIANS AND THE DARBYITES.

I had designed, on this occasion, to make a sect closely resembling the Plymouth Brethren, the Thomasites, or Christadelphians, my theme; a sect so little known that the very name, apart from a free translation, the Brethren of Christ, does not occur in the latest ecclesiastical authorities, and it was therefore with some curiosity that I reached Hooley's Theater, only to find that the meeting formerly held in its upper rooms was dissolved, and that this body now has no *ecclesia* in Chicago. This I regretted, since they are eclectic rather than the reverse, as their name might imply, and an exposition of the peculiar beliefs they entertained promised to be interesting. From a "Declaration of the First Principles of the Oracles of the Deity, set forth in a series of propositions demonstrating that the Faith of Christendom is made up of the Fables predicted by Paul (2 Paul iv: 4), and entirely subversive of the Faith once for all delivered to the saints," I learn their belief.

There will be a "Divine Political Dominion established on earth as the Kingdom of God

Jerusalem will be the Queen City of the World, the residence of the Lord Jesus, the headquarters and metropolis of the kingdom of God." This will continue for a thousand years, and be succeeded by the last judgment, when the approved will be immortalized, the wicked annihilated. Man's life, they claim, is merely mortal, the resurrection and consequent immortality, "immortality of life manifested through an undecaying body," only to be attained through Christ. Differing from the Plymouth Brethren in the above particulars, in their belief in the unity of God, though they recognize the preternatural birth of Jesus Christ, in their denial of the existence of hell and of a personal devil, for which they furnish biblical authority; they are one in church government, in the form of administration of the communion, and in the rigid excluness that distinguishes "saints" from all others.

Disappointed in this quest, I passed through the deserted streets of Chicago's business heart, and exchanging greetings with my friends the Hicksites on their way to meeting, entered an adjacent building where the Brethren gather. I had been led to believe that only brethren were expected to meet at the morning sacrament, that pleading was considered out of place in the assembly of believers, and that it was usual to preach in the evening only to such as were not converted. Happily my authority, noted light though he is, was at fault, and proof was offered at the outset that the little known, or supposed to be known about the Brethren, is inaccurate, an opinion which my later experience will confirm. I was kindly greeted, cordially invited to a seat, and found myself among the saints.

It was a comfortable room, with seating capacity for the two score assembled, occupying a double circle of chairs around an extension dining-table, on which stood a tumbler of wine and small loaf of bread, and the basket for offerings. The room was lighted on each side by windows looking out on a central court, used as a poultry-yard by a neighboring restaurant.

Hymns and prayers by different brethren alternated with long wedges of silence given up to silent prayer and meditation. During prayer some kneeled, some stood, others simply bowed the head, as inclination dictated. An hour passed, and the meeting so far resembled an ordinary prayer-meeting, without a chairman and lacking in zeal. But glancing around, and noticing the wrapt expression of each face, who but saints, thought I, could remain oblivious of such unyielding seats, such a babel of cocks crowing, ducks quacking, rattle of spoons, and clatter of dishes from court-yard and restaurant, fidgeting of little ones and hushing by mothers, or fail to see how slowly the sunbeams crept down the well-like walls toward us. Truth seemed in very deed to lie at the bottom of a well.

They seemed happily unmindful of these various discomforts, their heads bowed in thought, or elevated, with fast-closed eyes, until their faces were parallel with the horizon. A people of strong convictions, good foreheads, small noses, many with ruddy locks (but not, forgive the pun, Sandemanians), opposed to Malthusian doctrines, if the fact that one-fourth of our number were babies in arms, or little children, may be considered evidence.

The hymns were all old ones, of the time when general application was encouraged, before the Bliss and Sankey era had introduced the I and Me, the egotistical and personal form of appeal.

As the hour closes the cloth is removed, a short prayer uttered, and the Lord's Supper shared by all the saints; close communion is observed, the brother on my right rising as plate and goblet successively reach him, and carrying them round me to the sisters on the other side. A white-haired old man rises at its close to tell of a case of destitution which he has thoroughly investigated, in which a hard-working woman, outside of their community, has struggled, until overcome by sickness, to maintain her children and drunken husband, refused all aid by Roman Catholic relatives unless the children are resigned to them.

The day's collection, originally designed for the support of worship, is voted for this purpose, and as we leave each approaches the table and contributes to the fund. Before breaking up, a letter is read from a missionary laboring in that benighted region, New Jersey, who reports the accession of a Methodist clergyman and his entire family, speaks of the salary due his convert, withheld by his former flock for his apostasy, of the violent opposition he himself encounters, and adds, " But this is the way of the world, the religious world. Thank God, we are not of it! " concluding with love to the saints.

I am favored with pamphlets and tracts, from which, and subsequent conversation and inquiry, I condense the following facts regarding this little known body. So little known that it is popularly yet erroneously considered to hold the apostolic doctrine of community of goods, and its very title is a misnomer. They accept the name under protest, use it only with the article, " The Plymouth Brethren," deeming it like the term Darbyite, a vulgar appellation, and speak of themselves only as the Brethren.

They accept no written creed, encourage entire freedom of belief, yet hold to the doctrine of total depravity, the necessity of regeneration by the Holy Spirit, and atonement by the sufferings and death of Christ. Originating in Dublin in 1829, it was two years later before the congregation was formed in Plymouth, which speedily numbered 1,500 persons, and finally separated into Darbyites and Newtonites. When Darby subsequently expatriated himself to Switzerland, the work throve there, and his principles are the substantial basis of nearly all the so-called free evangelical associations of Italy. The first society was simply a gathering of Christians for religious improvement, who adopted the principle that they were free to celebrate the Lord's Supper without the help of any ordained minister; but did not separate themselves from the churches of which they were members, and some of their present ministers in England are members of the Established Church.

The Bethesda society established near Bristol in 1832, retains similar views, and their trust in the power of prayer for the supply of temporal necessities is nobly exemplified in the person of their leader, George Muller.

They believe that sectarian divisions are so many indications of the ruin of Christianity; that believers should withdraw from them, "and meet in separation from all ecclesiastical mummery." Rejecting any special ordination of the ministry, they consider all true Christians are priests, and authorize such to preach and administer sacraments, without further ordination than proof of their being found able to edify the brethren: regarding the work of pastors and evangelists as distinct, they allow payment of the latter while itinerating, but consider the payment of the pastors unscriptural. The sacrament is with them a weekly rite; and adult baptism is held to be of such moment, that, although not a condition of membership, members are usually re-immersed.

Although Darby's strictures were directed principally against the Church of England, he is accepted as authority by the Brethren to-day, and a revised edition of his pamphlets is laid under contribution for the following summary.

While the aims and purposes of believers are

very mixed in their nature, and fall far below the standard for which God has gathered them, and which He proposed as the influential object of their faith, and consequently as the motive of their conduct, division and sectarianism are, even in the mercy of God's providence, the necessary result. To suppose unity when the Church falls entirely short of the just consequences of its faith, is to suppose that the spirit of God would acquiesce in the moral inconsistency of degenerate man, and that God would be satisfied that His Church should sink below the glory of its Great Head, without even a testimony that He was dishonored by it.

When it was utterly sunk in apostasy, he raised his witnesses, yet still it was manifestly united with much that was merely human. This gave to the church a character which many discerned to be short of that which was acceptable to God. These observations are applicable to all the great national Protestant bodies, since the outward form and constitution became so prominent a matter, which was not the case originally while delivery from popery was in question. From this has followed an anomalous and trying consequence— that the Church of God has no avowed communion at all. The bond of communion is no longer the unity of the people of God, but, in point of fact, their difference.

It is not a formal union of the outward professing bodies that is desired. The life of the church and the power of the Word would be lost, and the unity of life utterly excluded.

Hence he deduces that one who seeks the interest of any particular denomination is, so far, an enemy to the work of the spirit of God, and that those who believe in the power and coming of Jesus, ought carefully to keep back from such "an unchristian spirit."

What we must fight against is the "practical spirit of worldliness in essential variance with the true *termini* of the gospel, the death and coming again of the Lord Jesus."

Would we be united, he argues, it must be the work of the Holy Spirit, and be indicated by growing, positive separation from all church bonds, and by "universal subjection to the Spirit, as our great, peculiar and proposed safeguard and strength."

Inviting no publicity, seeming to court obscurity, with no positive dogma, the distinction between a Plymouth brother and other sects, or, as he would say, the sects, is hard to define; but it may be summed up in the fact that every sec-

tarian difference is wrong, since division is wrong.
This, and a firm reliance on the Bible as the
Word of God, constitute all that they require
" to walk in the light as God is of the light," and
to have fellowship one with another.

AN OBSCURE DISEASE.

AN OBSCURE DISEASE.

Digest below from a contribution of Mary Boole, relict of George Boole, to a recent number of the *Athenæum*, may interest many other readers, who would doubtless welcome, as I should, any further information relative to the Rev. T. Everest or George Boole, and the views they held in the matters touched upon. This I ask for editorially, or from some of your valued correspondents, if you consider it of sufficient interest to accord the necessary space.

Somewhere between the years 1837 and 1843, my father, Thomas Everest, rector of Wickwar, in studying what is called occult science with the aid of a celebrated physician, made the discovery of a certain obscure disease, which, when it attacks persons of low animal organization, shows itself in a depraved taste for unseemly conversation about human relationships; if it happens to infect a man or woman of fine spiritual type, it takes the form of a desire to pry into the relations of man to the invisible. This seems to have been known to Jewish prophets from very early times; but I have some reason

to think that my father and his medical teacher
were first led to perceive it owing to the simi-
larity of the reactions of certain drugs in the two
cases. My father studied the subject closely. In
1851 he endeavored to call attention to it in a
sermon preached in London; but, of course, at
that day he was obliged to use carefully veiled
language. He was treated by medical men as a
fanatic, and theologians called him an atheist.
The world was not ready for his doctrine. He
endeavored to teach his family as much as he
could; we should, however, have understood him
better had he not kept us almost as carefully
shielded as the children of Jonadab, the son of
Lechab, from contact with the tendency against
which he uttered so many warnings. No "theology" was allowed to enter our house, nor any
novels or magazines in which it was alluded to.
But I remember enough of his teaching to have
grown to understand it later in life with my husband's help. Mr. Everest considered it especially sinful to attempt to convert a Jew to any
Gentile form of Christianity, and said that the
Jews as a body are destined ultimately to understand Jesus in a way of their own. When I asked
him what our church means by calling Christ
'God,' he seemed anxious to make me drop the

subject. He said: 'He is a manifestation of God; you are a manifestation of God yourself.' He forbade my seeking any other explanation, and at different times told us that Christ is our master; that whenever we can find out what his words mean, we ought to obey him literally, regardless of consequences, so we shall come to as much knowledge of God as is good for us; and that those who seek to find God in any other way than by such obedience, bring on themselves physical and moral injury.

Dipsomania and kleptomania are recognized terms employed to temper the disgrace brought upon decent families by scapegrace (scapegoat) relatives. Is it not high time that Spiritualists diagnosed a "certain obscure disease," if it exist, and thus account for our Sheas, Blisses, and other persons of low animal organization, barnacles on the good ship *Progress* ?

L'ENVOI.

L'ENVOI.

Of those who, in their various ways,
Give to Creation's Lord the praise—
Of folk devout, whate'er their creed,
    Right gladly do I sing:

But not of deeds of high emprise,
Nor yet of wasted human lives,
To gratify the ambition
    Of tyrant prince or king.

But of those who patient thrive,
Who still humbly live and strive,
Content that, in His own time,
    Their God will to them bring,

For their labors due reward;
That when over them the sward
Its mantle of true charity
    With tender hand will fling,

Christ will say, to their award
They have gone with conq'ring sword,
The grave hath won no victory,
    Death had for them no sting!

And I pray, when I too wait,
Expectant near Heaven's gate,
I may hear the anthems chanted
  By the great encircling ring

Of the seraphs, who, in state
On the great Jehovah wait,
Singing sweet praise ever
  To their Prophet, Priest and King.

www.ingramcontent.com/pod-product-compliance
Lightning Source LLC
Chambersburg PA
CBHW032111010726
47493CB00008B/2541